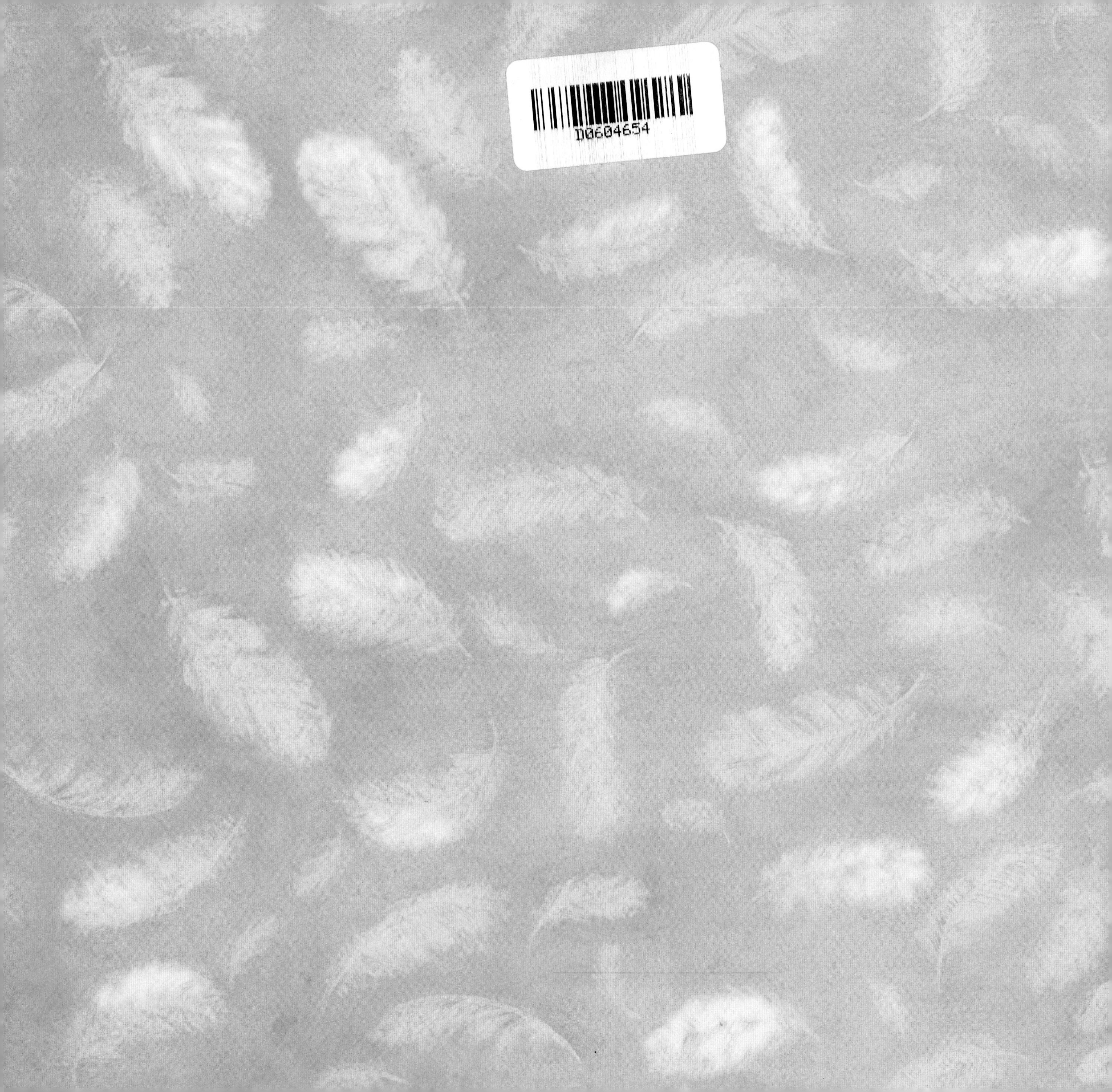

SHIVERHAWK

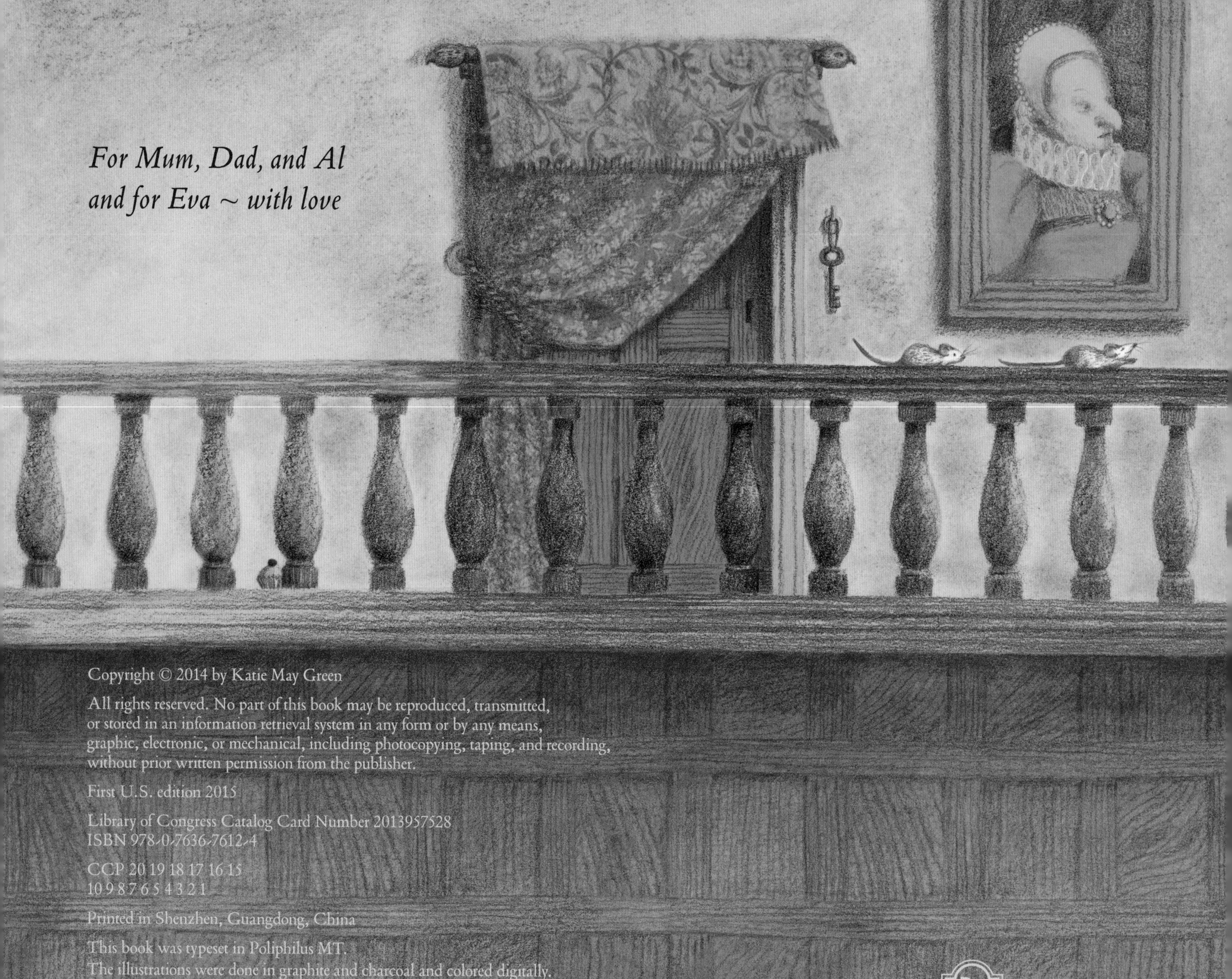

For Mum, Dad, and Al
and for Eva ~ with love

First U.S. edition 2015

Library of Congress Catalog Card Number 2013957528
ISBN 978-0-7636-7612-4

CCP 20 19 18 17 16 15
10 9 8 7 6 5 4 3 2 1

Printed in Shenzhen, Guangdong, China

This book was typeset in Poliphilus MT.
The illustrations were done in graphite and charcoal and colored digitally.

Candlewick Press
99 Dover Street
Somerville, Massachusetts 02144

visit us at www.candlewick.com

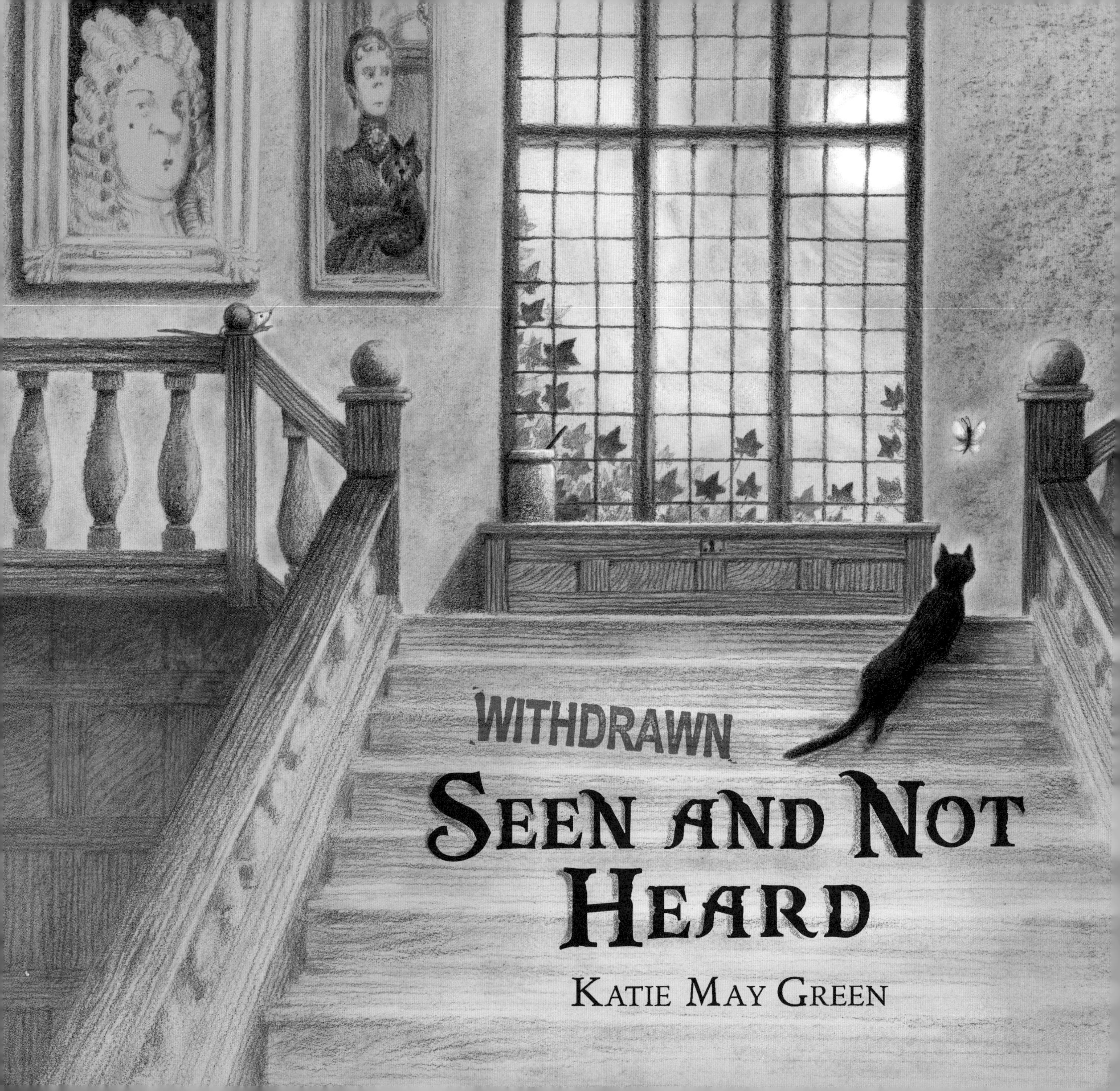

Seen and Not Heard

Katie May Green

In a big old house, up creaky stairs,
in a silent little nursery full of dolls
and teddy bears, you'll find the children
of Shiverhawk Hall.

They're children in pictures on the wall—
seen and not heard.

LILY PINKSWEET
BILLY FITZBILCIAN III
PERCY PINKSWEET
Prudence, Peter, and Pearl Plumsey
Lila and Vila DeVillechild

Lily Pinksweet
Billy Fitzbilgian III
Prudence, Peter, and Pearl Plumsey

Don't they look so sweet and good,
so well behaved,
as children should?

There's little Lily Pinksweet,
a dainty delight,

and the Plumseys, so grown-up,
their manners so polite.

Billy Fitzbillian is the cleverest boy,

Percy is the kindest —
he'll share any toy.

And as for those twins,
the DeVillechild girls, they are . . .

PERFECT

ANGELS.

But how do they feel in their picture
frames when their frocks tickle and
their collars prickle and their noses
itch and they mustn't scratch?
How can they stay so still
and good, sweet little children,
just as they should?

Well, when the night is whispering
and the moon is high,
when there's no one to see them,
when there's no one to spy,
carefully they creep, nice and quiet . . .

PERCY PINKSWEET
BILLY FITZBILLIAN III
Lila and Vila De Villechi

and the Shiverhawk children

all run RIOT!

They race down the hallway, giggling with glee!
"I'll be the leader," says Lily. "Follow me!"
"Midnight feast!" says Percy. "Ooh, goody, goody, goody!"

And they gallop to the kitchen, shrieking,

"Yippeeeeeeeeeeeeee!"

Starting with dessert
is Percy's favorite way to dine.
"Get your paws off
my trifle," he says.
"It's MINE!"

Catching cakes in her
mouth is Lily's best trick.
Sticky ringlets,
jammy ribbons,
fizzy tummy . . .
"I feel sick."

The Plumseys leave
the pantry,
carrying pots of
treacly goo.
The others hop
from foot to foot:
it's time for
something new.

"Let's do some painting!"
Lily says with a twinkle
in her eye.
"That's the way to
do it!" says Billy.
"Dip, slick, a lick,
then dry!"

The fun spins onward,
upward, faster,
louder, higher!
Breathless bouncers
whirl and hoot.
Happy hearts
flip and fly!

And then . . .

pillows burst . . .

and giddy laughter softens into silence,

floating,

fluttering

in the air.

"The moon is getting tired," says Lily.
"Let's get back before the sun!"

And hearing Lily's warning words,
the children start to run.

They race along the hallway and run up the creaky stairs,
back into their nursery, to their dolls and teddy bears.

LILY PINKSWEET
BILLY FITZBILLIAN III

"Oh, no!" says Lily Pinksweet
as she climbs into her frame,
for she sees that Percy's missing,
not in place above his name.
"Come on, Percy, hurry!
You're running out of time!"

And just as the sun creeps in
the room . . .

they're all back.

They stay still and sweet and good,
just as children should.

Lily Pinksweet
Billy Fitzbillian III
Percy Pinksweet
Prudence, Peter, and Pearl Plumsey
Lila and Vila De Villechild

Seen and not heard.

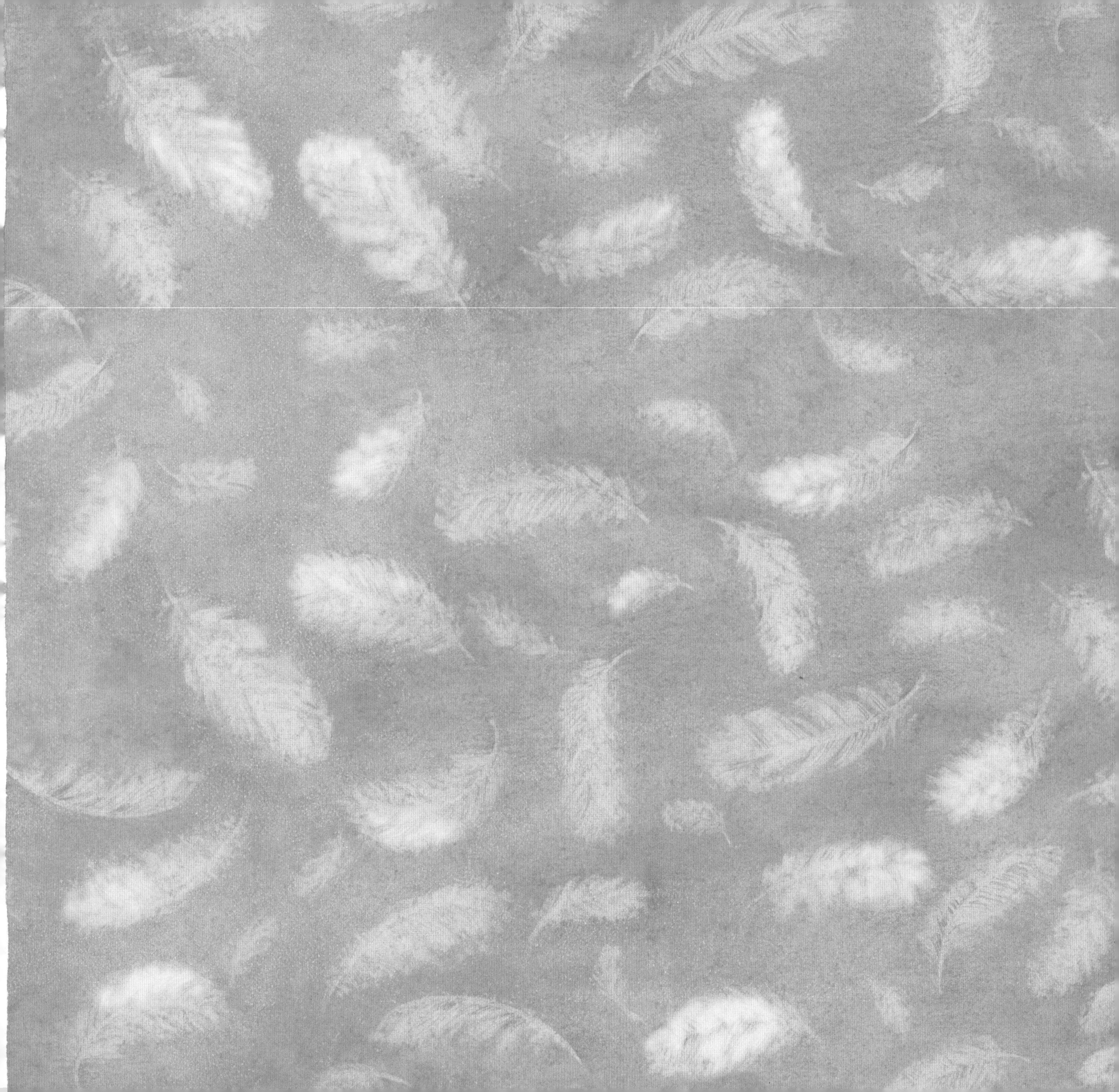

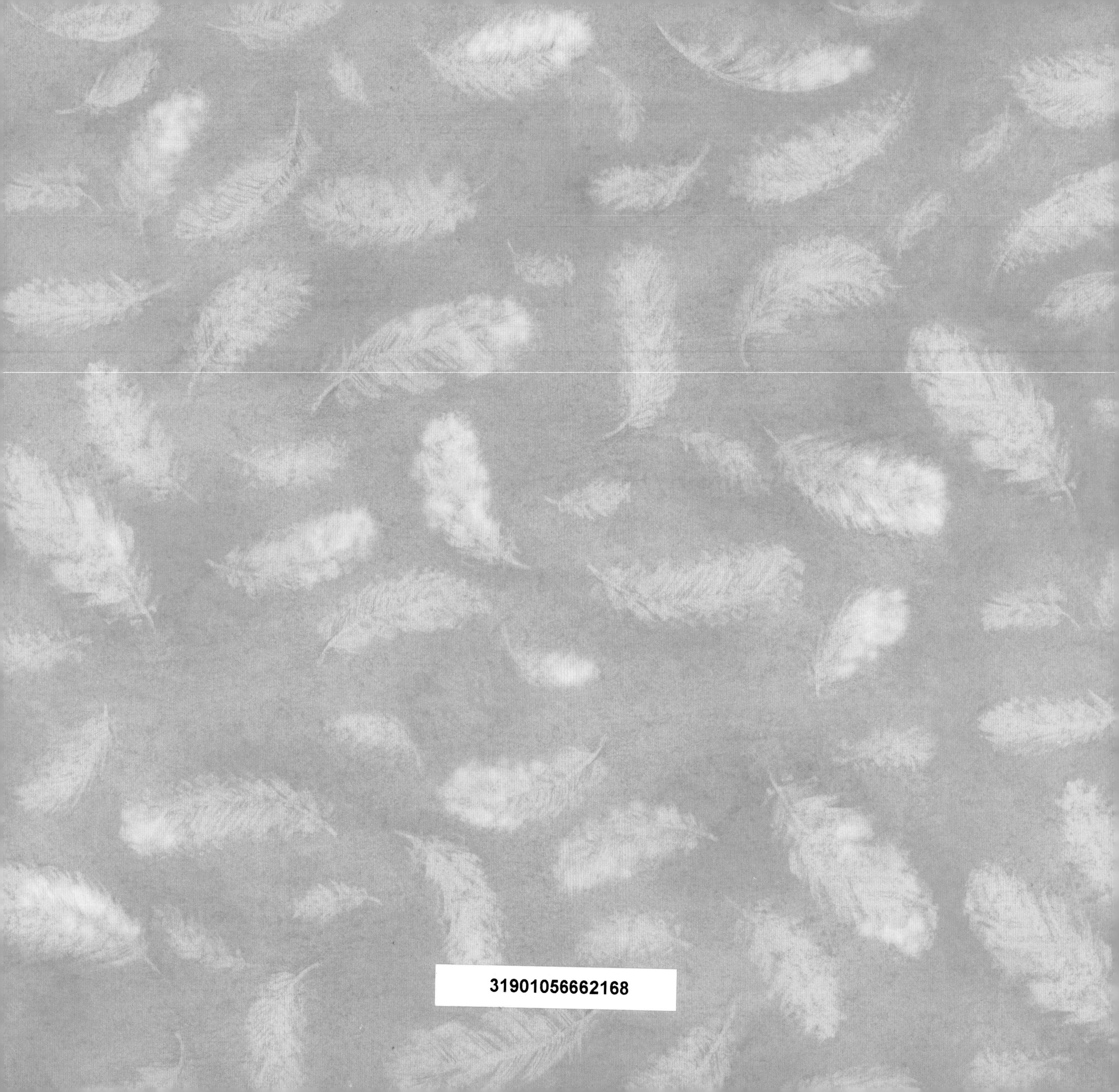